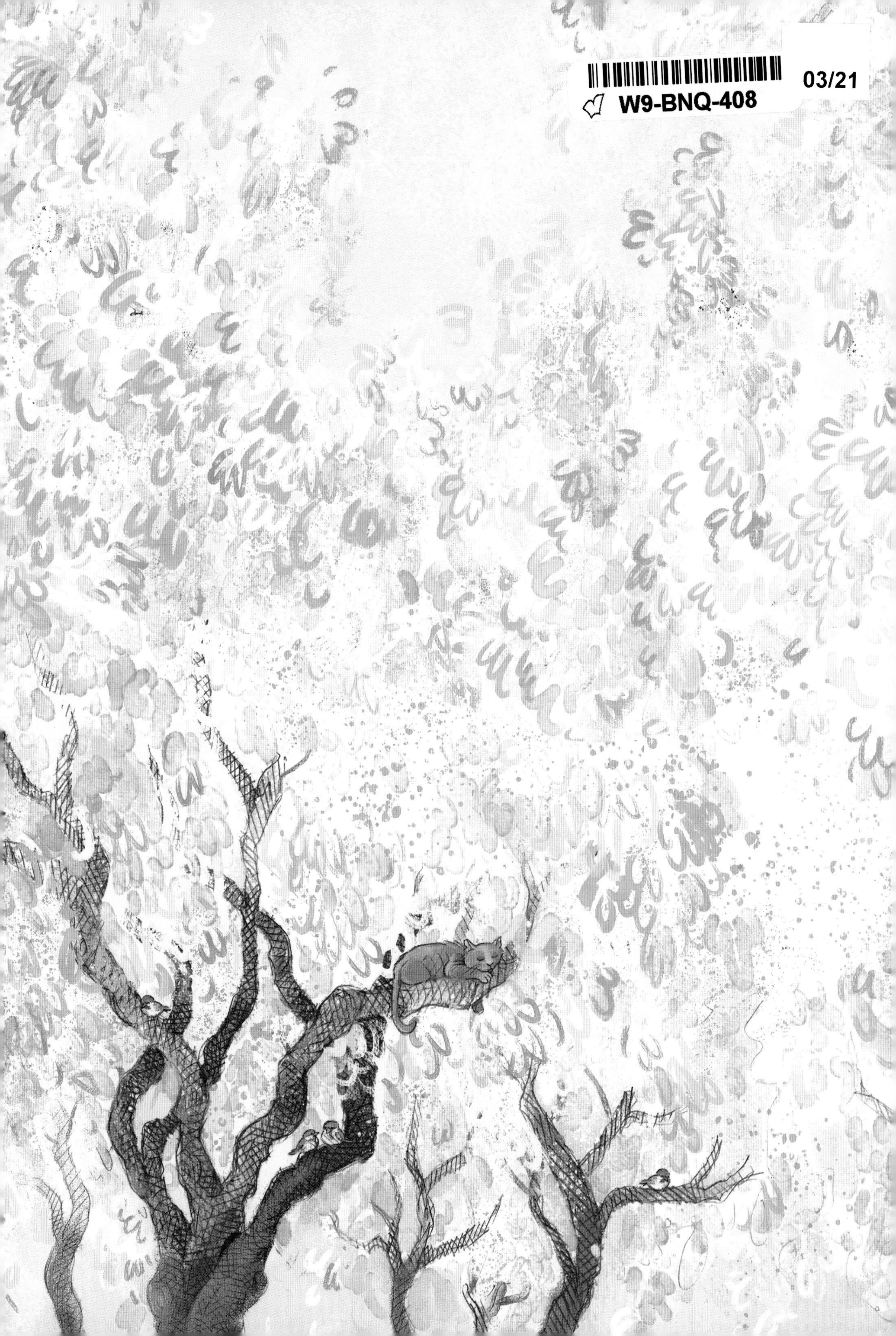

The
Passover
Guest

ADAPTED FROM
Der Kunzen-Macher (The Magician)
by I. L. Peretz

Susan Kusel

Illustrated by
Sean Rubin

NEAL PORTER BOOKS
HOLIDAY HOUSE/NEW YORK

Muriel loved Washington in the springtime. The white buildings stood out crisply against the green lawns. The cherry trees burst into pink blossoms at the Tidal Basin. She could feel Passover in the air.

The year 1933 was different.
Her father, like so many others,
had lost his job. Her family
didn't have enough to eat even on ordinary days. It would
be impossible to buy all the food needed for their Passover
seder. They didn't even have enough wine to fill the
ceremonial cup for the prophet Elijah, who was said
to visit every Passover seder.

So there was no need to rush home to prepare the holiday feast. Muriel walked slowly from the park and stopped to look up at Lincoln on his magnificent marble chair.

A strange figure dressed in rags, juggling on the steps of the monument, caught her eye. He looked as threadbare as the men on the street waiting in line for soup.

As she watched, his brown hair turned red. The eggs he juggled became blazing candles. His shabby clothes turned into those of the finest silk.

Muriel was amazed. She took
her only penny and put it in
the hat at the man's feet.

He smiled at her. "The sun is
setting. Passover is about to start.
You don't want to miss your seder."

"My family isn't having one this
year," Muriel answered.

"Are you sure?" asked the man.
"Perhaps you'd better hurry home."

He sounded so confident
that Muriel started walking,
quicker than she ever had before.
She ignored the Washington
Monument, gleaming in the
fading sunlight.

She rushed past the White House
without a second glance. Gradually
the stately buildings began
to recede.

When she got to her neighborhood, her stomach grumbled as she smelled the delicious food from other seders. The celebrations were smaller this year, but she could still see tables filled with food and windows shining with light.

What could the man have meant? How could they have a feast without any food? Her feet went faster and faster.

When she arrived home, she opened the door in anticipation. But she only saw the same shabby room with the spindly chairs and rickety table that had always been there. Her parents emerged from the shadows dressed in their best clothes for the holiday, even though there was no food on the table, no gleaming silverware, no wine set aside for Elijah.

"Every door will be open to us on Passover," said her father. "Let us find another home where we can celebrate."

As Muriel reached for the door handle, there was a knock. When she opened it, she saw the mysterious stranger standing there. "May I join your seder?" he asked.

"You are welcome to share anything we have," answered Muriel's father. "But this year, we have nothing."

"I have everything we need," said the man.

Muriel turned and looked again at the room. It was no longer shabby, but glowing with light from countless candles. The chairs were piled with comfortable pillows. And the food! There were mountains of tender brisket, oceans of flavorful soup, and fields of crunchy matzah. A magnificent seder plate lay in the center of the table, complete with an egg, a shank bone, horseradish, parsley, lettuce, and charoset.

There was even a beautiful cup of wine for Elijah. Muriel hadn't realized she was hungry, but now she wanted to eat everything, even the horseradish.

Muriel and her parents couldn't believe their eyes. After seeing so little food for so long, their house was now bursting with it.

"Can this really be?" her mother asked.

"How is this possible?" her father asked. He sounded nervous.

"Everything is possible on Passover," answered the man.

Muriel could tell her parents were uneasy. She volunteered to ask the rabbi if they could proceed with this astonishing meal.

She told him about their mysterious guest and how a magnificent feast had appeared from nowhere.

"If you can pour the wine and break the matzah, then what you have described is a true miracle," said the rabbi. "Can you show me your seder?"

She ran to the synagogue and found the rabbi about to start his own seder.

Muriel led the way, and the rabbi's curious guests followed. More people joined the procession as it passed other seders.

When they reached Muriel's house, the crowd
was enormous—but the stranger was no longer there.

Everyone crowded into
the tiny house. They all
managed to fit inside as
the rabbi examined
the table.

They watched as the wine poured
itself and then the middle matzah broke
in two and became the afikomen the
children would look for later.

The rabbi picked up a piece of matzah, crumbled
it in his hand, and then blessed the meal. "This is
not an illusion," he said, "but a Passover miracle.
We may all enjoy this beautiful feast."

There were enough chairs for all. Their own seders forgotten, the guests joined Muriel's family in their retelling of the story of Passover. They dipped their parsley in salt water and ate bitter herbs. Muriel asked the four questions about Passover. All the children searched for the piece of hidden matzah, which was found just before midnight.

Muriel realized that in all the excitement they had forgotten to open the door for Elijah. But when she looked at his cup, there was not a drop of wine in it.

Now she knew who the
mysterious stranger was.

אליהו

A Note from the Author

Passover has always been my favorite holiday, a time when I watch spring chase away winter. As a child, I loved assembling all the elements of a seder. The most important part was setting out a full cup of wine for the prophet Elijah. I always waited to see if he appeared and took a drink from it. Every year I felt that I would see him if I only tried harder.

When I was a child, my mother read me *The Magician* by Uri Shulevitz, an adaptation of I. L. Peretz's *Der Kunzen-Macher*. My favorite part was when a poor couple actually *met* Elijah. Decades later, I found the book again in a Jewish library, and I sank down on the floor and read it over and over, remembering how much I had loved the story.

This new version takes place during the Great Depression, a logical time in which to set a story about a desperately poor family. The United States experienced the worst of the Depression and its highest unemployment rates in 1933. This book is set on April 10th of that year, the first night of Passover.

I grew up in the Washington, D.C., area and have always loved its beautiful cherry blossoms. There are three thousand cherry trees planted around or near the Tidal Basin, a gift from the government of Japan in 1912. Every spring, these trees produce gorgeous blossoms and are visited by more than a million people. In 1933, the peak bloom coincided with the first night of Passover.

I have always admired the elegant and imposing Lincoln Memorial. It is a magnet for people all year long, but especially during cherry blossom season. In the original story, the magician is performing in a village square. The Lincoln Memorial has always felt like D.C.'s town square to me.

There is a rich history of the Washington, D.C., Jewish community, which began to form in the 1850s along 7th Street Northwest. In 1906, the Adas Israel congregation began to build a now-historic synagogue at 6th and I Streets, which was a functioning conservative synagogue in 1933.

Polish writer Isaac Leib Peretz originally published *The Magician (Der Kunzen-Macher)* in 1904 as a short story in Yiddish. Picture-book editions include the Shulevitz version I read as a child, as well as one by Barbara Diamond Goldin illustrated by Robert Andrew Parker, and even one with illustrations by the famous painter Marc Chagall.

A Note from the Artist

As a child, I was fascinated by the artist Marc Chagall. For one thing, he was one of the few Jewish painters anyone talked about. As a budding illustrator with Ashkenazi Jewish heritage, I noticed that. It didn't matter that I was also Italian American—Italian painters were a dime a dozen, so Chagall was my man. I displayed my "I and the Village" poster from New York's Museum of Modern Art prominently on my bedroom wall. I also liked that Marc Chagall illustrated books. Chagall created a handful of admittedly bizarre illustrations for a 1917 Yiddish version of I. L. Peretz's *The Magician*, the story that inspired the book you now hold.

If Susan Kusel's adaptation began as a love letter to the writing of I. L. Peretz, my illustrations soon became a tribute to the paintings of Marc Chagall. My style and Chagall's didn't have much in common, but as I began creating the illustrations for this book, I found his approach to color, lighting, and even some of his windows and chickens showing up on the pages. And although musical instruments are not used in some observant Jewish homes on holidays, in homage to Chagall, I included instruments throughout the illustrations to give a sense of the traditional songs that are an important part of Passover. What an honor it was to illustrate the same story, more than a hundred years later.

Passover is a story of faith—faith in the promise of a bright future while still contending with a grim present. I am reminded of this story every spring at my family's seder, but I am especially reminded as I write this note in the spring of 2020. As humanity prepares yet again for a struggle against plague and financial uncertainty, the message of Passover remains a light in darkness: evil comes and evil goes, but we're still here.

A Note on the Passover Holiday

Passover (Pesach) is an important Jewish holiday in the spring. It retells the story of the Jews' escape from slavery in Egypt and recounts several events from the Book of Exodus in the Torah. It is observed in the home with an event called a seder, which is a combination of a religious service and a festive meal. There is usually a seder plate on the table, which holds many of the traditional symbols of Passover. Charoset is a combination of apples, nuts, and wine, which is symbolic of mortar used by the Jewish slaves in Egypt. The shankbone symbolizes the Pascal lamb, and the egg and parsley symbolize spring. The parsley is dipped in salt water to show the tears the slaves cried. Horseradish (bitter herbs) and lettuce (chazeret) are also echos of the bitterness of slavery. The youngest child asks four questions about how Passover is different from all other nights, which are answered during the seder. Because the Jews did not have enough time for bread to rise when they were fleeing Egypt, flat crackers called matzah are eaten during Passover. The afikomen is a piece of matzah that is hidden in the house for the children to find for dessert.

Elijah is a famous Jewish prophet who is said to be the one who will announce the coming of the Messiah. A traditional part of a Passover seder is opening the door for Elijah. There are many stories in which Elijah grants miracles and riches to those who are generous and welcoming.

Author's Acknowledgments

With thanks to Wendy Turman of the Lillian and Albert Small Capital Jewish Museum,
Michelle Eider of the Sixth & I Synagogue, Danielle Winter, Rabbi Amy Schwartzman, Rabbi Jeffrey Saxe, and
Rabbi Stephanie Bernstein for their guidance; Rabbi Laszlo Berkowits for his assistance with the Yiddish translation,
the Temple Rodef Shalom community, Maria Salvadore, Susan Polos, Wendy Stephens, Amy Forrester, Hena Khan,
Liza Parfomak, Madelyn Rosenberg, Anamaria Anderson, Mary Ann Scheuer, Heidi Rabinowitz, Kathy Bloomfield,
Alison Morris, Chava Pinchuk, Alex Zealand, Annie Lechak, and my friends and writing groups for their help;
Ken, David, Matthew, Dan, Lorraine, Russ, Ava, and Andrew for their amazing support;
Jennifer Browne for her design work, Marietta Zacker for her guidance,
Sean Rubin for his beautiful illustrations, and Neal Porter for everything.

To my family—the magicians in my life —S.K.

For my parents —S.R.

Neal Porter Books

Text copyright © 2021 by Susan Kusel
Illustrations copyright © 2021 by Sean Rubin
All Rights Reserved
HOLIDAY HOUSE is registered in the U.S. Patent and Trademark Office.
Printed and bound in September 2020 at Toppan Leefung, DongGuan City, China.
The artwork for this book was created with graphite on Bristol board
with digital color and additional line work in Adobe Photoshop.
Book design by Jennifer Browne
www.holidayhouse.com
First Edition
1   3   5   7   9   10   8   6   4   2

Library of Congress Cataloging-in-Publication Data

Names: Kusel, Susan, author. | Rubin, Sean, 1986– illustrator.
Title: The Passover guest / written by Susan Kusel ; illustrated by Sean Rubin.
Description: New York : Holiday House, 2020. | "Neal Porter Books." |
Summary: In Washington, D.C., during the Great Depression, Muriel and her
family have no money to prepare the seder meal until a mysterious stranger
performs a Passover miracle. Includes notes on the Passover holiday, the
Great Depression, and the history of the D.C. Jewish community.
Identifiers: LCCN 2019010711 | ISBN 9780823445622 (hardcover)
Subjects: | CYAC: Passover—Fiction. | Judaism—Customs and
practices—Fiction. | Jews—United States—Fiction.
Depressions—1929—Fiction. | Washington (D.C.)—History—20th
century—Fiction.
Classification: LCC PZ7.1.K89 Pas 2020 | DDC [E]—dc23
LC record available at https://lccn.loc.gov/2019010711

ISBN 978-0-8234-4562-2 (hardcover)